The Mystery of the Disappearing Egyptian Reports

The Two Brothers Series, Volume 1

Muhammad Zaid Bilal

Published by Muhammad Zaid Bilal, 2024.

This is a work of fiction. Similarities to real people, places, or events are entirely coincidental.

THE MYSTERY OF THE DISAPPEARING EGYPTIAN REPORTS

First edition. April 18, 2024.

Copyright © 2024 Muhammad Zaid Bilal.

ISBN: 979-8224834402

Written by Muhammad Zaid Bilal.

Table of Contents

Special thanks to my parents and teachers

The Two Brothers Series

THE MYSTERY OF
THE DISAPPEARING EGYPTIAN REPORTS

M. ZAID BILAL

THE TWO BROTHERS SERIES
THE MYSTERY
OF
THE DISAPPEARING
EGYPTIAN REPORTS
M. ZAID
BILAL

The Mystery of the Disappearing Egyptian Reports

By Muhammad Zaid Bilal

Index

FOREWORD

Welcome to my debut book, The Mystery of the Disappearing Egyptian Reports. As I embark on this literary journey, I am filled with both excitement and a sense of responsibility. I chose to write this book with a specific purpose in mind. My aim is to showcase the richness of Pakistani culture and heritage through the lens of a captivating mystery set in Marsala Village, Hyderabad. Amidst the pages of this story, I hope to highlight the values of modesty and integrity while addressing the challenges posed by the prevalent immorality and vices in our society. While crafting this narrative, I found myself immersed in the vibrant tapestry of our culture, drawing inspiration from the beauty of our traditions and the resilience of our people. It is my sincere hope that readers will not only enjoy the thrilling plot but also gain a deeper appreciation for the values that underpin our society. I welcome your feedback and suggestions for improvement. Please feel free to reach out to me at zaidbilaliqbal@gmail.com. Your insights will be invaluable as I continue to refine my craft and embark on future literary endeavors. Thank you for joining me on this adventure. Until we meet again in the pages of my next title, adieu.

Warm regards,

Muhammad Zaid Bilal.

MR. ASAD'S SECRET

It was a typical Sunday night and Ahmed was getting ready to sleep. He was a fourteen-year-old boy who had a reputation for being too curious. Living in the Eastern part of Marsala Village, he soon became a nuisance for the village policeman, Mr. Salem Khan, or Mr. Khatarnak, as everyone liked to call him. He had just changed into his night clothes and was checking if the windows were bolted when he heard an uproar. 'A strange noise', he thought. "It's coming from the direction of Meezan Bank", he said to himself. At first, he thought that he had just imagined it. However, when he saw a strange red glow from the Bank, his worst fear was confirmed.

He quickly roused his sleepy brother, "Hasan, wake up. Wake up! There's something quite strange." Hasan sat upright, groaning. He was a year younger than his brother and liked to mind his own business. Nevertheless, his brother seemed to have the ability to always persuade him to accompany him on his adventures.

"What is it?" Hassan said sleepily. "Looks like a blaze to me." They both looked out of the window.

"Yeah, it is something on fire. *Inna lillahi WA inna ilaihi rajiu'n*[1]. I say we go see what it is."

Not bothering to change their clothes, lest they should miss the chance, the two of them ran down the stairs. Their

---

[1] Verily, we belong to Allah, and verily we shall return to Him.

father had not locked the door yet, so they dashed out of the house.

Following the crowds of people running wildly towards the blaze, they reached the site of the fire. As they tried to jostle their way to reach the front ranks, they made out the burly figure of Mr. Khatarnak. Upon spotting them, he said, "Get out of here, you brats. You've got no right poking your heads into the police's business." He wanted to pounce on them but the front line blocked his view. Disgusted, he abandoned his intention and focused on the blaze instead. He ordered, his mouth towards the people, "Back off! Don't get near it."

The screeching of fire engines were heard in the distance. Soon, the firefighters had taken charge. They were constantly aiming streams of water at the blaze. The people watched dumbfounded as the roaring flames started to lose color and steadily diminish. Even Mr. Khatarnak, oblivious to his duties, watched relieved as the flames turned into a heap of burning firewood. The water from the huge extinguisher gushed out and sprayed the blaze until it turned into tiny whispers of smoke. Finally, the blaze was completely out.

The next moment was a shock to everyone. Mr. Asad, a middle-aged man, dressed in a coat and suit jostled his way through the crowd and ran blindly towards the bank, until he was a yard behind the debris. Mr. Khatarnak stretched his hand out and caught him with the front end of his garment, that brought him back to his senses.

"I have got papers in there, real, invaluable, original documented papers."

"They are quite invaluable to me. They contain all my life's work," said Mr. Asad.

. Ahmed was standing calmly in a corner, unnoticed by the crowd who were too absorbed; he was studying Mr. Asad. He had stepped up from the front ranks, revealing his brother and himself, and said, "And may I enquire what the work is?".

Mr. Asad paused before answering, to study the newcomers. Fooled by their childish looks, he replied quietly, "You come to my residence after this."

He also handed the brothers his card when nobody was looking. Aloud, he said, "Mind your own businesses." Mr. Khatarnak added his favorite words, "Get out of here, you brats."

"Sorry sir, but we need to carry out all legal proceedings before you can reclaim your papers."

"Uh, ok, I shall go home. You tell me when your work finishes." He added with a smile, "So that I can continue with mine."

The crowd dispersed. The policeman started searching for footprints and testing for fingerprints. He also roamed around the vicinity in an attempt to find any clue to aid him in his investigation. Meanwhile, Ahmed and Hasan returned home.

The next morning, the boys decided to visit Mr. Asad.

They wanted to find out about the secret of the papers.

Mr. Asad's house was nothing short of a mansion. It had the most modern technology that the villagers could afford. It even had solar panels.

Hasan remarked, " What a spectacular house!

Allahumma Barik."

Ahmed also busied himself studying the grandeur of the house that presented itself.

"Assalamualaikum." Mr. Asad's husky voice brought the brothers out of their daydreams. They returned the greeting.

Mr. Asad led the brothers through a spectacular passage into his grand living room. Mr. Asad took a seat at one of the old mahogany chairs and gestured to the brothers to take one each, as well.

"Well, I think maybe someone is jealous of me. It all started two days ago when I received some spiteful letters. As you know, I am a scientist and my study revolves around ancient treasures, so it was natural that someone had an eye on my work. Recently, I had written an archeology report about where the ancient Egyptian treasures were located. The report also listed scientific methods for searching for those. So, the sender, whoever he was, indicated that he wanted the report, whilst I had no particular intention of publishing it. I just kept it in Meezan Bank for safekeeping.

But yesterday's incident, you know, means that somebody has taken it."

"Did you discuss that report with anybody?" asked Ahmed.

"Um, no, well except that I was talking with the government officials one day. That too was in my own house," he replied. "I don't see how anyone could have overheard me."

"Okay, can you please take us to the room in which you had that conversation? By the way, when did this happen?"

"It only happened two days before yesterday, on Monday. In the morning, I was talking to the officials. In the evening, I received the first letter," said he.

"Do you mind if we take a look at the spiteful letters after we've seen the room?" asked Hasan.

"No, not at all. Anyways, I think you're um, are you investigating the case?" he asked.

The two brothers glanced at each other and then Ahmed decided to speak, "Yeah, we thought that...."

"Okay, okay, I understand." Mr. Asad replied. "Here is the room."

They were standing in a spectacular study, lit by fluorescent bulbs on all four walls. There were many shelves lined up against the wall. On one side was a small armchair against a mahogany desk. Mr. Asad had lined his books up neatly onto his desktop. The room overlooked the garden.

There was a small window in that direction. The boys took a look at the window and asked him, "Can anyone stand in there and overhear the conversation going on in here?"

"I do not think so, but you can investigate. If that can help find the person who was constantly threatening me, I shall help you in every possible way." he replied.

"Okay, I shall go out into the gardens and you both talk about anything as if I am not there. I shall see if I can overhear you through the window," said Ahmed.

"Okay, let me take you to the garden." Mr. Asad said.

The brothers followed Mr. Asad to the garden, amidst pleasant fragrances and spectacular corridors. It was well-kept and the grass was mown equally, resembling the work of a talented craftsman. There were all sorts of flowers; marigolds, roses, sunflowers, daffodils, daisies etc.

After Ahmed took his post at the window, Mr. Asad went back into the study with Hasan. Hasan's mind was racing. He thought about what to talk about.

At last, they reached the study. Hasan found Mr. Asad an easy person to talk to. They talked about all sorts of things like Badminton, cricket, cooking, life etc. After five minutes of this discourse, Ahmed gestured through the window.

Soon, Ahmed joined them again. He told Mr. Asad that it was easy to overhear the conversation that was going on inside. He looked startled.

Mr. Asad left to find the letters. Ahmed and Hasan, in the meantime, started to discuss their case. They talked about how they were going to list all suspects and investigate their alibis one by one.

Soon, their host returned with the letters. They were neatly piled up. Ahmed took a letter at random. It read:

Dear Mr. Asad,

You will never find me, be sure of that. I have heard all about your report on the treasure, so be quick. Slide it under your door the first thing in the morning. Don't think of calling the police.

Yours.

"Excuse me, Mr. Asad. I just wanted to ask you a final question." Ahmed said.

"Go on, I shall not mind," he said.

"Do you know of someone who probably would have done this? Anyone in particular?" Ahmed asked him.

"Well, um, yah, I think. You see, I don't trust those two neighbors of mine. And I cannot also vouch for you know Mr. Arif. He's quite strange." he responded.

LOOKING FOR CLUES

After Mr. Asad's house was well out of sight, Hasan asked Ahmed, "Where are we going now?"

"Well, first we shall go to our house. We shall disguise ourselves and then go to the bank." Ahmed replied.

"Why will we disguise ourselves? Can't we go into the bank in our original get-up?" Hasan asked.

"You know, the thief might be lurking inside. We don't want him to know that we are working on the case." Ahmed replied.

They entered their house in time to see their parents going out. They asked the boys to remain at home in their absence.

"Don't worry," said Ahmed. "We won't be going out anywhere until you return."

"We are going to the supermarket. It won't take us more than half an hour."

The boys took advantage of the leisure time they got to disguise themselves. They took out all sorts of fake moustaches and smeared their faces with make-up. By the end of this, they could not even recognize themselves.

Ahmed looked like an old man. He had wrinkles on his face and was wearing spectacles. Hasan, on the other hand, looked like a small boy, energetic and lively, wearing a blue casual shirt and a neat khaki lower.

"Now, listen to the plan. I am Naranjo, your grandfather and you are going to be Bahadur, my grandson. OK?" said Ahmed.

"OK. I shall comply."

"Don't forget to call me Dada." "OK, I am not a kid."

Soon, their parents came home and the boys left towards the bank. On the way, Ahmed admonished Hasan not to give away their real identities.

"So, Bahadur, if you feel that we are being suspected or watched by any person, just leave that activity of yours. We shall just snoop around a little and gather as many clues as we can, OK?"

"OK, I shall do that, Brother." "Call me Dada, Bahadur." "Oops! Sorry, Dada."

As the boys neared the bank, Ahmed told Hasan to remain quiet. They tiptoed in as to not give themselves away. Inside, the debris was neatly piled up at the side. As expected, there was no one at the bank save Mr. Khatarnak.

Upon noticing the boys, he shouted, "Get out of here, you brats."

They complied without objection. Mr. Khatarnak was bewildered but he decided not to show it to the boys.

On the other hand, the boys stopped as near as they could without giving themselves away. They discussed the plan in hushed voices.

"Bahadur, we shall wait until Mr. Khatarnak leaves the vicinity, then we shall enter. OK?"

"Yes, Dada."

"And we are going to start with the back of the bank where the vault is. Next, we are going to check all the counters..."

Hasan pinched Ahmed. He pointed towards the Bank from which Mr. Khatarnak emerged.

After Mr. Khatarnak was out of sight, the two brothers tiptoed towards the bank. As discussed, they searched the vault but to no avail. Next, they started searching behind and beneath the counters. Ahmed took the left side while Hasan took the right side.

Suddenly, a shout emerged from Hasan's mouth. He called to see what he had found. There was a little pass-port size photograph of Mr. Asad behind one of the counters.

"Good job, Bahadur," Ahmed interjected. He pulled out his notebook and wrote:

Clues

1.   Small photograph of Mr. Asad

They searched for more clues, but found none except a Gold Leaf cigarette butt and a handkerchief with the initials A.B inscribed on it. Ahmed jotted both of them in his notebook and carefully tucked the cigarette butt and the handkerchief in his pocket. Ahmed glanced at his watch. It was 8:45 a.m.

"Bahadur, it is getting late." Ahmed said.

As they exited the bank, Hasan asked his brother, "Where are we going, now?"

"To Mr. Arif's house."

They drove towards Mr. Arif's house, which was located in the dingiest neighborhood, FACH. This neighborhood was considered a notorious hideout for thieves, murderers, and other criminals. Mr. Arif lived alone. Only his housekeeper-cum-guard accompanied him. Ahmed parked the car outside Mr. Arif's chamber.

It was the most dilapidated house the brothers had ever seen. The boys took off their make-up and knocked the door. After a minute or two, the housekeeper opened it and led them through a feeble staircase up to his employer.

Mr. Arif was a man of around sixty years old. He had a white moustache and a beard of the same color. He was bald except for two lines of hair on both sides of his head. He wore baggy trousers and a plain white kurta.

Ahmed introduced himself and his brother to Mr. Arif. "It's good to see youth after a long time" said Mr. Arif.

"Do you mind if we ask you some questions?" asked Ahmed.

"Regarding what?" asked Mr. Arif sharply. "About the recent blaze in Meezan Bank."

Upon hearing this, his face relaxed. "Go on, son." "Where were you at the time of the blaze?"

"At my home here."

"Then how did you get to know about the fire?" "Through the newspaper." He replied.

Ahmed felt inclined to believe that what the old veteran said was true. He asked his permission to search the house.

"No problem. I am glad if that helps find the arsonist."

So, Hasan and Ahmed searched the grounds. They found no imprint or clue. When they were departing, Ahmed had a great idea.

"Mr. Arif, do you know something about the initials A.B?"

"Those are my initials, Arif Bhatti. Where did you find them?"

"In the bank."

"I think someone is trying to frame me." Mr. Arif cried. "We hope we'll find them soon." Ahmed replied.

Ahmed and Hasan departed. When they reached their car, they found one rear and one front tire punctured.

"A puncture," Ahmed said angrily, "Wait until we catch the criminal, then we'll give him tough time."

Anyways, they went to the nearest mechanic and asked him to repair the puncture. Soon after, they were racing towards Mr. Asad's house, and subsequently, his neighbors".

After an hour or so, they were able to reach Mr. Asad's mansion. They rang the doorbell and were immediately taken to the living room. Mr. Asad was anxious to hear the developments of the case. After being seated at the luxurious sofas, Ahmed began, "We have rightly taken a look inside the bank, and have found your photograph…"

Mr. Asad interrupted, "It must have fallen off the papers!" he exclaimed.

Ahmed produced the photograph and Mr. Asad confirmed his claim. "We have also found a handkerchief with the initials A.B and a Gold Leaf cigarette butt," Ahmed said, producing both. He also told him about their experience at Mr. Arif's house. Upon the end of Ahmed's tale, Hasan showed him their diary.

Mr. Asad, after reading its contents, asked about the new course of action.

Ahmed told him about his intention to visit the neighbors. Mr. Asad was satisfied and wished them good fortune. The brothers, then took permission to leave. Mr. Asad waved them goodbye.

AT THE NEIGHBOURS'

After a few moments, they were at Mr. Shariq's house. Before they advanced their hand towards the doorbell, the same thought crossed their minds.

"What preliminary would we offer?"

Nevertheless, Hasan reached out cautiously towards the bell, which was surrounded by a maze of possibly unearthed wires. Before, he could ring the bell, a strong masculine voice greeted him.

"Mr.Shariq?" Hasan asked politely, turning towards the source of the voice.

Mr. Shariq was a muscular man, with broad shoulders and a protruding chest. His countenance, however, wore a broad smile, revealing his clean, white teeth. His almond-shaped eyes seemed the perfect welcome to the brothers. Before beckoning them inside, he asked his wife to observe the Islamic veil. After seating them in his lounge, which was very accommodating, he asked his wife to bring the guests some tang, despite their repeated "no, thank you"s.

After she served them each a glass full of tang, Mr. Shariq came straight to the point. "What brings you here?" He asked.

Ahmed briefed him about their progress, leaving out Mr. Asad and Mr. Arif's part of the tale, lest they alert him if he proved to be the criminal. Mr. Shariq sipped his tang thoughtfully, then replied, "Ah, I see. You two are working to catch the arsonist of the bank."

Ahmed nodded in agreement. Mr. Shariq denied having any more information than what was evident from the boys' tale.

After extracting no other clue from Mr. Shariq, Ahmed asked him, "May we talk to your wife to see if she can provide us with any more information?"

Mr. Shariq replied, "I doubt whether she could help you in any way. You know, she rarely ever goes out of the house."

Anyways, he asked his wife to come in. She sat by her husband's side, obviously disturbed by the strangers' presence in her house. The brothers also sensed this.

They asked her their usual questions. They learnt that the couple was in their house, sleeping when the incident happened, and only got to know about it the next day through the Express Daily. The brothers felt inclined to cross the couple off their list of suspects. Realizing that further questioning was futile, they bade the couple "Allah Hafiz" and left.

Dejected that their first visit bore no fruits, the two approached Mr. Asad's other neighbor, Mr. Asif. They had to knock the unpolished mahogany door, as Mr. Asif's house had no doorbell. As the brothers waited to be answered, they took a look at the house. It was very small, a beetle in front of Mr. Asad's mansion, just short of a cabin. The desolate state spoke multitudes about the financial conditions of its owners. It could serve as a spooky haunted house or as a perfect hideout for criminals. Ahmed saw much reason why anyone like Mr. Asif would be the perfect person to get his hands on a valuable report, though he did not see his advantage in bringing the bank down.

Mr. Asif opened the door and admitted the boys. He was a man around 60, almost similar to Mr. Arif, except that he had a smaller beard. His house was spick and span. It seemed that despite their financial crisis, his wife had taken good care of the house.

Mr. Asif ushered the boys into his bedroom, since he had no other place to offer them. He asked the boys to feel home. After making themselves as comfortable as they could, they started to question the person before them. He briefed him about their purpose, to which he responded positively. Mr. Asif, to their joy, revealed that he had seen the security guard talk with a masked person, the other day. Just then, Ahmed took a look at his watch. It was half-past nine. They were expected to be home by then. They hurriedly bade the veteran farewell and returned to their house, just in time to hear their mother ask them to come for dinner.

Their father joined them on the dinner table, a moment afterwards. They informed their family about their progress. Their father, Mr. Ahsan, to their surprise, did not object. Their mother, on the other hand, asked them to remain cautious and not to run themselves into danger.

"Don't worry," said Ahmed, kissing his parents goodnight. "Shab bakhair," said their father.

The next morning, the brothers rose early feeling rejuvenated and energized. After praying their dawn prayers, they are a light breakfast of eggs and milk and sought their parents' permission to resume their detective work. Their father admonished them to remain safe and also offered to, drive them to their destination. The brothers respectfully declined the offer and set off.

After a few minutes, they were at their previous destination. They knocked on the door and were greeted by an excited Mr. Asif. He asked his wife to observe the veil and admitted them to his bedroom. Ahmed hurriedly apologized for their departure the previous night. After the usual discourse, they resumed their 'investigation' .Mr. Asif denied having any knowledge of the incident, neither did his wife. They shook their heads and reiterated their support.

Mr Asif said, "We're extremely sorry. We never go to a bank. However, we still extend our warmest support to you."

Hasan nodded in agreement and showed his inclination to believe the couple. Ahmed, contrarily, felt less convinced. He asked," Do you receive the morning paper?"

Mr. Asif replied in the negative and was close to tears. Ahmed, realizing his mistake, apologized without delay. The brothers bade the couple farewell and exited their dilapidated yet kept residence. They felt no hindrance in crossing the couple off their list of suspects.

The brothers then decided to report their progress to Mr Asad. They approached his mansion and were surprised to see him walking up and down the street, his countenance a pungent shade of chlorinated yellow-green. As he saw the brothers, his face relaxed.

He quickly ushered the boys inside, and got straight to the point. "Thank God, you are here. I almost thought that you had forsaken the case. Tell me what happened."

The boys informed him about the progress. He seemed satisfied and placid. He offered to make them coffee, but they respectfully declined. As they were about to leave, they heard a loud knock on the front door.

ANOTHER ANGLE

The boys rushed to open the front door. As they stood there gazing through the blinding sunlight, they could only make out the form of a burly figure turning round the street corner. At the doorstep, they found an envelope. They delivered it to Mr. Asad.

Mr. Asad ripped off the seal and found a letter inside. He dismissed it as a regular letter of a friend and dismissed the matter. The boys left his mansion.

As soon as they reached their house, their mouths dropped. They found the front door open.

"It is unlike Ammi to leave the door open like that," said Ahmed.

The boys rushed inside the house, only to find all family members safe and sound. They learned that their mother was in a hurry and her hands were laden, so she could not shut the door.

After heaving in a hearty brunch, the boys rushed to their room to discuss their progress. It seemed like all their resources were exhausted and they were still at zero. All suspects were crossed off their list, and they had reached a dead end.

Hasan opened his notebook for the umpteenth time. Finding no clue, he banged it on his head in frustration. He expected no success. Ahmed, on the other hand, frantically racked his brains to find an unexplored angle in the case.

Suddenly, he had an idea.

'Hasan, look how stupid we are! We just disregarded Mr. Asad himself."

"You mean to say that Mr. Asad might be making a phony story all this time?"

Ahmed nodded in agreement.

'But how do we know whether Mr. Asad is guilty?' asked Hasan.

Ahmed reminded him of the spiteful letters Mr. Asad had handed them, the day they had started on the case. The brothers planned their next move cautiously, as to not alert the criminal.

The boys sought their parents' permission to be late for dinner. They were surprised, but did not object, as they had no complaints about their sons.

The boys immediately started off on the clue of the letters. First, they approached Mr. Arif's house, as the houses of all other suspects were in the same vicinity.

Their car chugged along the dilapidated neighborhood, which looked a little lively due to the onset of the national elections. Within a few minutes, the boys had reached Mr. Arif's house. They knocked the door, and were almost instantly greeted by Mr. Arif's guard. The guard had a frown on his face. The brother asked about his employer, to which he angrily replied, "Dead. He has died, poor man.

Don't know it?"

The brother felt sorry for him. They could fully understand the impact of the bereavement on the guard. They offered him their condolences and prayed for the deceased.

Realizing that their presence would further increase his agitation, the boys immediately bade him goodbye and left towards the next suspect.

They knocked at Mr. Asif's door. After a few moments, Mr. Asif's wife asked, "Who's there, and what do you want?"

The boys told her that they were from the neighboring area and wanted to speak to Mr. Asif.

The lady replied that her husband would return in the evening by 5pm. The boys did not object.

They directed their vehicle to Mr. Shariq's house. Fortunately, he was home. He greeted the boys with a wide toothy grin.

"You've become as rare as the 'Eid crescent," he remarked.

Nevertheless, he offered him the best hospitality he could. His wife had already observed the Islamic veil, and was in her room. Mr. Shariq ushered the boys into the lounge, and offered them beverages. Despite their repeated attempts to respectfully refuse, he took out cold drink cans from the refrigerator and placed them in front of his guests.

He then came straight to the point, and asked them the purpose of their visit.

Ahmed began, "You see, it's been a long time, and still the bank arsonist isn't caught. So, we were asking if you would permit us to go through some of your banking history."

Surprisingly, Mr. Shariq did not object. The boys asked for a written approval, so that the bank would not refuse their request. He quickly wrote a short note, and signed it. The boys took an oath to not handle anything unlawfully. Mr.

Shariq seemed satisfied.

The boys then went to the bank with Mr. Shariq's written approval. The bank had temporarily shifted its operations into the secondary branch.

The banker seemed suspicious, following the boys' request, but after he confirmed with his client, he allowed them to see Mr. Shariq's banking history supervised by the branch manager. The boys looked at the recent cheques. They compared his handwriting to the handwriting in Mr. Asad's letter. There was a stark difference. The sender had a cursive style, but Mr. Shariq had a plain, simple print-like font. They thanked the bankers for their cooperation and headed back outside.

Ahmed glanced at his watch. It was a quarter past five. They decided to pay a visit to Mr. Asif, before Mr. Asad.

As expected, Mr. Asif was home and expecting them. As soon as they knocked on the door of his house, he let them in. The boys quickly briefed him about their progress, and humbly requested samples of the couple's writing.

'Sorry, but I don't know how to read and write. You see, I never got to learn it."

For his wife, he offered to give them her diary, but the boys gently refused. They took a few photographs from various pages of the diary, and returned it to the man.

On their way to Mr. Asad's house, the boys compared Mrs. Asif's writing to the script on the letter. Although both of them were written in a cursive font, the diary was more legible, and less stylish. Meanwhile, the letter resembled a page from the register of an untidy student. The formation of letters was entirely different in the diary and the letter.

Soon, the brothers reached Mr. Asad's mansion. Little did they know that they had a surprise waiting for them.

VICTORY FOR JUSTICE

Mr. Asad sat the brothers comfortably in his conspicuous drawing room. His housekeeper brought them cold beverages, on his employer's orders.

After the boys had drunk their beverages, Mr. Asad delved straight to the point. He inquired about the developments on the case. Ahmed excused himself, and exited the room, while Hasan started briefing Mr. Asad right from the beginning.

Ahmed, on the other hand, dialed the police helpline and put the phone on speakers. He had convinced the superintendent to not show his presence on the line, lest Mr. Asad was alerted.

Ahmed returned with the phone in his hand. Meanwhile, Hasan had done good not to let Mr. Asad know that the suspicion landed on him. All went smooth, until Ahmed asked a witty question, albeit casually, "Mr. Asad, I say could you spare us a sample of your writing?"

Mr. Asad turned pale, but recovered almost instantly. "What for?" he retorted.

"We just needed to check whether your writing matches the one on the spiteful letters." Ahmed said calmly.

The sirens of police mobiles were clearly audible now.

As soon as Mr. Asad heard the sirens, he dashed towards the door, but Ahmed had already taken care of that. Soon, there was a loud thud on the door. The police superintendent bellowed, "Open up!"

Despite, Mr. Asad's resilience, Ahmed managed to unlock the door. The superintendent walked in, followed by other police officers and a sulky Mr. Khatarnak.

Mr. Asad protested, "You cannot barge in like that. It's private property!"

The policemen offered no sympathy to the man and handcuffed him behind his back.

The superintendent neared Mr. Asad and looked straight into his eyes.

"It's better if you come clean, Asad. Otherwise, we shall use the iron fist."

Seeing no chance of an escape, Mr. Asad confessed his crime.

"I admit faking the letters to throw these boys off my trail."

"And made a phony story about the Egyptian reports, to get my hands on the bank money." The superintendent finished for him.

Mr. Asad was put in a police mobile, and driven to the police station. Soon, he was behind bars.

A huge ceremony was held to congratulate the valor of the boys, at the village hall. The President handed over medals of bravery to the boys and the whole village gave them an ovation. They had made their parents and their fellow villagers proud.

That night, before they slept, Ahmed remarked to his brother, "Phew, it ended up, alright. *Alhamdulillah*"

"I'd rather hope this one is the last one for a long time," Hasan sighed, sleepily.

The boys turned on their right sides and recited their prayers. They slept almost instantly, oblivious of their surroundings. Little did they know that they would be soon engaged in another mystery, "*The Labyrinth Museum*

Mystery."

About the Author

Muhammad Zaid Bilal is a passionate writer with a knack for crafting captivating mystery fiction. With a background in creative writing, Zaid draws inspiration from his surroundings and his love for storytelling to create gripping narratives that keep readers on the edge of their seats. When he's not writing, Zaid enjoys teaching and playing cricket. 'The Mystery of the Disappearing Egyptian Reports' is his debut novel, showcasing his talent for weaving intricate plots and engaging characters.

Read more at https://www.upwork.com/freelancers/~01407cdd7c0bf5380e.

About the Author

Dorothy Abasola

Dorothy Abasola was honored by the grand champion in the field of writing and songwriting.

Writing has been her way to alleviate her sadness and impatience during her time abroad. She has also written many different life stories and her children were inspired by these stories to learn how to live a life where there is no hope other than God.

Became a contributor and editor of SENTRY at Bulacan Polytechnic College, Graduated Bachelor of Arts in English Communications.

For her you will not know something if you do not try it and "Success is liking yourself, liking what you do, and liking how you do it."

"Commit to the Lord whatever you do and He will establish your plans"

www.ingramcontent.com/pod-product-compliance
Lightning Source LLC
Chambersburg PA
CBHW021325160726

47994CB00004B/1613